Herodotus was a young hedgehog,
curious about everything.
He loved wandering through the gardens
and the meadows and the forest
that surrounded them.

Jean-Luc Buquet

Herodotus
the hedgehog

Eerdmans Books for Young Readers
Grand Rapids, Michigan

"How interesting!" said Herodotus.

There was a bee caught in a web
          and a spider was rushing toward it.

Watch out, little bee! thought Herodotus.

"Phew," sighed Herodotus. "He escaped!
That's very interesting!"

Suddenly, Herodotus heard the deep voice of a bear rumbling nearby.

"Oh, Mighty Bear Spirit, who protects us, who makes us strong, please accept this fruit and honey."

The bear left his offering at the foot of the tree
and began to dance around strangely,
raising his front paws up toward the sky.

Herodotus was fascinated.

"That's incredibly interesting," he said.
"I love fruit, and honey too."

And Herodotus quietly walked away.

"Hello, Hedgehog!"

"Hello, Fox."

"Why are you all curled up like that?"

"Oh . . . you never know."

"Are you afraid of me?"

"No! Well . . . maybe a little."

"Relax, I've already eaten."

"What did you eat? Or . . . *who?*"

" . . . I ate my fill."

"You know, I saw a bear just now.
He was talking to a tree."

"To a tree? Maybe he's a little crazy.
Or perhaps he was just lonely."

"I don't know. He was saying 'Mighty Bear Spirit,
who protects us, who makes us strong,
please accept this fruit and honey.'"

"And he was dancing all around, like this,"
Herodotus added.

"You're funny, hedgehog!"

And the fox continued:
"It's the same with us, though. We have
our own Great Spirit—the Great Fox.
It is said that she sometimes appears
with her two daughters, Wit and Prudence."

"Ah!"

"But others say that it's just a story for young foxes,
and they don't believe it."

"Ah!"

The two sat quietly for a while,
looking up at the sky.

Herodotus was good friends with an old hedgehog.

He was a little gruff, but also old and wise, so all the hedgehogs respected him and called him Venerable.

"You seem deep in thought today, Herodotus,"
said Venerable.

"I was wondering . . . do we have a Great Spirit,
like the bear and the fox do? Is there a
Great Hedgehog Spirit?"

"Your mother didn't teach you about that?"

"She died when I was very young."

"Hmm . . . yes . . . well then . . . a Great Hedgehog Spirit? You see, we hedgehogs are humble creatures. Since the beginning of time, we've only known one thing—though it's a very important thing: the sun rises, and then it sets."

"That's it?"

"That's huge!"

He's getting really old, thought Herodotus.

"I'm going to ask all the animals!" Herodotus declared.
"The sheep, the rabbit, the otter.
The deer, the donkey, the ox.
They're big animals—they must have
fascinating Great Spirits!
And maybe I'll ask the ants, and the fish in the creek too.
But not the badger or the owl . . . they might try to eat me."

And all of the animals told Herodotus
about their Great Spirits.

The weasel started.

"I have to say, the finest Spirit of all
is the one who created weasels. We're very
smart. Not like those poor sheep!"

The sheep said,

"Our Great Spirit gave us the gift of love!
We are peaceful. And no one wants to stand out.
What's good for one sheep is good for the flock.
And we don't eat our neighbors!
We're too modern for that!"

The wolf said,

"Look at them! Those sheep don't have
a Great Spirit like ours—proud, fierce, free!
But they are charming . . . I do like them quite a lot."

Hoopoe said,

"Hoop! Hoop! Hoop! Great Bear, Great Fox—
what nonsense! There's only one Great Spirit,
who made every single one of us, whether
beaked or toothed, furry or feathered."

"Really?" asked Herodotus.

"Yes, the Great Spirit created you and me both,"
said the hoopoe. "Whenever we sing
with all our might, from the top of the tree
to every corner of the world—the Great Spirit is there."

"Only one Great Spirit?"
murmured Herodotus.

"Unbelievable, isn't it, Hedgehog?"

It was Raven.

He added, "Personally, I think your Great Spirit is completely made up."

"*Hoop! Hoop! Hoop!* I'm not going to discuss this with you," said the hoopoe.

"Okay, okay. But you did make him up, didn't you?"

"You're nothing but a stupid clod!" the hoopoe said

Hoop! Hoop! Hoop!

Caw! Caw!

They argued for a long time,
    and then flew off and disappeared.

There was a great silence in the forest.

There was a great silence in Herodotus's head.

He closed his eyes.

Bear, Fox, Weasel, Sheep, Wolf, Hoopoe, Raven . . .
their voices all swirled around in a great storm
in Herodotus's head.

And then there was silence again.

Little lights danced behind his closed eyelids.

He felt his heart fretting a bit,
carried by a wave of concern and hope.

"Is that you, Great Hedgehog?" Herodotus asked timidly.

The silence was suddenly broken by crying,
singing, the flapping of wings.

A gentle breeze caressed Herodotus.

"I am a hedgehog," said Herodotus the hedgehog.
"And I'm hungry—hungry and thirsty!"

He felt the light fading in the forest,
and then he heard the sound of footsteps.

He opened his eyes.

Venerable was there.

They looked at each other for a moment.

Then Herodotus said,
"I understand, I think.
Let's go see the sunset."

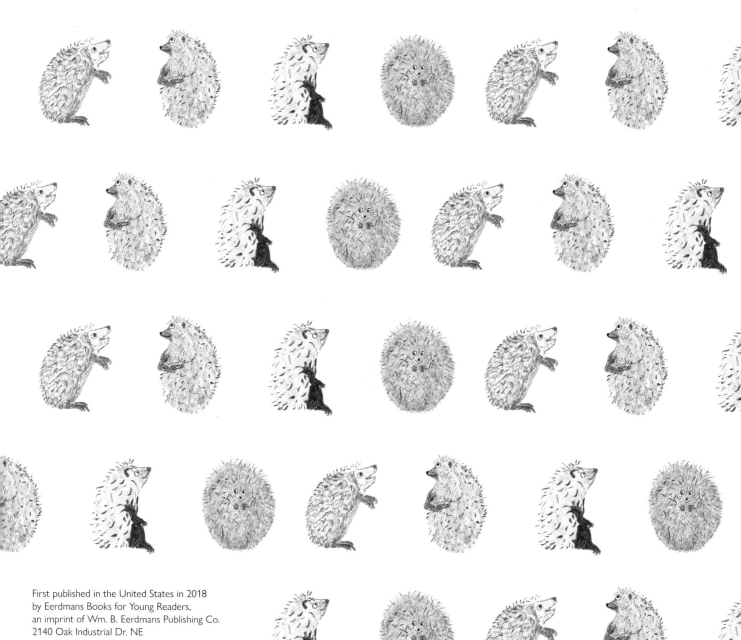

First published in the United States in 2018
by Eerdmans Books for Young Readers,
an imprint of Wm. B. Eerdmans Publishing Co.
2140 Oak Industrial Dr. NE
Grand Rapids, Michigan 49505
www.eerdmans.com/youngreaders

Originally published in France in 2015 under the title
Hérodote le hérisson
by Éditions courtes et longues, Paris
Text and illustrations by Jean-Luc Buquet

Manufactured in China.

26 25 24 23 22 21 20 19 18   1 2 3 4 5 6 7 8 9

Library of Congress Cataloging-in-Publication Data

Names: Buquet, Jean-Luc, author, illustrator.
Title: Herodotus the hedgehog / by Jean-Luc Buquet.
Description: Grand Rapids, MI : Eerdmans Books for Young Readers, 2018. |
   Summary: "A curious hedgehog asks the other forest animals what they
   believe in, but he eventually needs to choose his own beliefs"— Provided
   by publisher.
Identifiers: LCCN 2017031269 | ISBN 9780802854988 (hardback)
Subjects: | CYAC: Faith—Fiction. | Curiosity—Fiction. | Hedgehogs—Fiction.
   | BISAC: JUVENILE FICTION / Visionary & Metaphysical.
Classification: LCC PZ7.B915326 Her 2018 | DDC [E]—dc23 LC record available at
https://lccn.loc.gov/2017031269

The illustrations were created with oil paints using a monotype printmaking technique.